Brother Bartholomew

and the APPLE GROVE

Brother Bartholomew
and the APPLE GROVE

Jan Cheripko • Kestutis Kasparavicius

Boyds Mills Press

Published by Boyds Mills Press, Inc.
A Highlights Company
815 Church Street
Honesdale, Pennsylvania 18431
Printed in China

Publisher Cataloging-in-Publication Data (U.S.)

Cheripko, Jan.
    Brother Bartholomew and the apple grove / Jan Cheripko ; Kestutis Kasparavicius. —1st ed.
[32] p. : col. ill. ; cm.
Summary: An ambitious monk learns a lesson in humility when he encounters
Brother Bartholomew, the old monk who tends the apple grove.
ISBN 1-59078-096-5
1. Humility — Fiction — Juvenile literature. 2. Monks — Juvenile fiction.
3. Orchards — Fiction — Juvenile literature. (1. Humility — fiction. 2.
Monks — Fiction. 3. Orchards — Fiction.) I. Kasparavicius, Kestutis.
II. Title.
   [E] 21   PZ7.C54Br 2004
2003111534

First edition, 2004
The text is set in 12-point Stone Serif.

Visit our Web site at www.boydsmillspress.com

10 9 8 7 6 5 4 3 2 1

For my friend, Father Stephen Morris
—J. C.

For my son Tomas
—K. K.

ONCE, NOT SO LONG AGO, HIDDEN HIGH ON A GREEN HILL overlooking a blue river curled in the valley below, stood a saintly monastery. Even though the monastery stretched far across fields and woods, only eight monks tended the sheep and harvested the apples, berries, beans, and corn each fall.

The brothers spun the wool into sweaters. They crushed the berries into jams and jellies. And they pressed the apples into creamy applesauce. Each year, the monks had just enough money from the sweaters, the jams, and the applesauce to pay the bills.

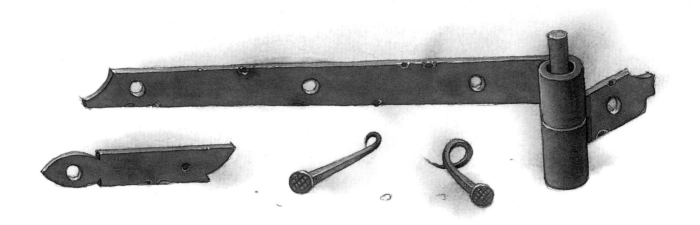

The work was hard, but the monks loved their simple lives. Still, they were getting older, and it wasn't as easy to do the many chores that had to be done. For years, Brother Bartholomew tended the apple trees. Poor Bartholomew—his rheumatism was so severe he hobbled with a cane when he walked. Despite his pain, Brother Bartholomew worked hard, but sometimes, if the truth be told, he didn't close the gate to the apple grove. The monks couldn't be sure if he forgot or simply didn't close it because the gate was too heavy and the hinges were broken. Sometimes they would close it for him, and sometimes, they were just too tired to close the gate.

Whether Brother Bartholomew left the gate open or closed didn't matter to the deer. The fence was so old and rickety the deer could easily jump over it, or in some spots, walk right through its huge holes. When the monks questioned Bartholomew about the open gate or the unrepaired fence, the old monk would smile and say, "God will provide."

The monks didn't want to hurt Brother Bartholomew's feelings. He had tended the apples for more years than anyone could remember. Quite frankly, there were so many things to do at the monastery that no one else had extra time to care for the apple grove anyway. And each year there did seem to be enough apples to make the applesauce that kept the monastery going.

One day, a new monk arrived at the monastery.

Brother Stephen was young and strong. He was hard-working, too. The first time he saw the deer in the apple grove, he was appalled. The deer were feasting on the apples while Brother Bartholomew sat in a chair. Brother Stephen wasn't sure if the old monk was praying or sound asleep.

Brother Stephen marched up to Brother Bartholomew and said, "Brother Bartholomew, the deer are eating all the apples."

Brother Bartholomew looked up slowly. "Oh, yes, the deer," he said. "Yes, yes, the deer are eating the apples."

"I know that," snapped Brother Stephen. "How will the monastery survive if we don't have enough apples?"

Brother Bartholomew smiled. "God will provide," he said. "He always does."

Indeed, there were enough apples that fall to make the applesauce. The monastery survived another year—just barely. All winter long, Brother Stephen couldn't stop thinking that if he took care of the apple grove he would fix the fence, build it higher, never sit in a chair to watch the deer, and he certainly would never leave the gate open. The deer would never get in to eat the apples, so there would be more money from the applesauce. And if the monastery had more money, the monks could pay their bills, fix up the chapel, buy a new bell, and even build a new guesthouse.

Once the thought had entered his mind, it seemed as though all Brother Stephen could think of was how he could tend the apple grove better than Brother Bartholomew. Soon that one thought became many thoughts; and then images flooded his mind. Brother Stephen could see himself fixing the fence, harvesting the apples, and getting praise from the other monks for his hard work. Surely there could be nothing wrong with working hard to help the monastery?

"Shouldn't monks be free from worldly worries?" Brother Stephen would ask himself. "Of course, they should," he would answer. "If only Brother Bartholomew would hurry up and . . ." Brother Stephen tried to stop himself, but the thought slid into his mind like a new key into a lock. " . . . and die!" The word clicked in his mind and locked down deep in his heart. Brother Stephen swore to himself that he would never let that secret out.

Every so often, however, Brother Stephen would look up from his work (and his thoughts) and there would be Brother Bartholomew watching him. Brother Stephen would look into the sorrowful eyes of Brother Bartholomew. But he could not look for long. The key that had locked his awful thought in his heart would jiggle a little, but his heart remained shut.

In the spring, Brother Bartholomew grew ill. The monks knew that their beloved brother would soon die. One by one, each monk went to Brother Bartholomew's room to bid him good-bye. They sat by his bedside and wept, asking his forgiveness for any wrong they may have done to him. And one by one, Brother Bartholomew blessed them.

At last it was Brother Stephen's turn. How could he face Brother Bartholomew? But how could he face the monks if he did not go? Finally Brother Stephen, his eyes staring at the floor, found himself sitting by the bedside of old Brother Bartholomew.

"Brother Stephen," Brother Bartholomew whispered.

When Brother Stephen looked up into Brother Bartholomew's eyes, he quickly turned away because of his shame at having thought all those long winter months that he could tend the apple grove better if only Brother Bartholomew would die.

Brother Bartholomew knew the heaviness in Brother Stephen's heart. He reached his weak hand across to touch Brother Stephen and whispered, "God has forgiven you and so do I." Then he paused and said, "Tend my apples."

Brother Stephen's heart leapt with joy. At last he got what he wanted. He forgot Brother Bartholomew's forgiveness, and he didn't listen to Brother Bartholomew's warning: "You are a strong man and you will work hard for the apples, and that is good. But a man's strength is often his greatest weakness. Remember, God will provide."

Brother Bartholomew died that night.

The very next day Brother Stephen began rebuilding the fence around the apple grove. First, he fixed the broken hinges on the gate so that it would swing shut and lock itself. Then he put in new posts, fixed the holes in the fence, and built it higher and higher—and never sat in the old chair or left the gate open.

Day after day, the deer watched warily from the edge of the woods, eyeing the feverish work of Brother Stephen.

Day after long day, Brother Stephen stepped from his work and admired his grand fence, thinking of all the applesauce the monastery would now sell and all the great things they could now accomplish. How the monks would praise his hard work!

Brother Stephen looked up the hill at the deer on the edge of the woods, shook his fist at them, and yelled, "You're not dealing with old Brother Bartholomew anymore. Just you try to get into *my* apple grove!"

One fall morning, as the apples ripened and filled the air with their rich juicy smells, a huge buck stepped from the edge of the woods and stared straight down the hill at the apple grove. First, he looked at the fence, and then he looked at Brother Stephen.

Brother Stephen stared back. He saw the buck's fourteen-point rack of antlers covered in golden velvet, glimmering like a crown. Then he noticed how tall and muscular the buck was. Finally, he looked into the buck's deep brown eyes, haunting, beautiful, and somehow familiar.

The buck shook his massive head. The morning sunlight dancing on the tips of his antlers; the dew dropping like diamonds to the ground. Slowly the buck and Brother Stephen turned to look at the fence.

Brother Stephen knew what he had to do. He raced to the barn and pulled out two rolls of razor-sharp barbed wire. All day and all night he strung the rolls along the top of the fence, adding a foot or more to the top all the way around the apple grove. Even during lunch and dinner, which the monks had to eat together, and during the day's prayers, which Brother Stephen couldn't miss, all Brother Stephen could think of was finishing the fence. And he only half listened during the evening service when the Abbot read the passage about pride coming before a fall. By midnight he was done. A full moon was already past its peak in the sky when Brother Stephen, exhausted but proud of his long day's work, collapsed into Brother Bartholomew's chair. There he waited to see if that buck might still try to jump *his* fence.

The buck stepped from the shadow of the woods and into the moon-drenched field on the hill above the apple grove. The great buck snorted, pawed the ground, lowered his head, and raced down the hill toward the fence. In one magnificent leap, he bounded from the ground like an arrow from a bow. Up he soared, his great rack shining in the moonlight like a halo, his two front legs easily clearing the barbed wire.

Brother Stephen leapt from the chair, his eyes wide open and mouth gaping in disbelief.

But as the buck glided over the fence, raising his back legs up behind him, his right back hoof caught the barbed wire. Suddenly he was catapulting though the air like a giant stuffed animal. The buck crashed to the ground with a sickening thud.

For a long moment, neither Brother Stephen nor the buck moved. Then Brother Stephen walked slowly to the gate and unlocked it. The big gate swung shut behind him and locked. He walked cautiously to the animal lying motionless on the ground. The buck raised his head, breathed heavily through his nose, opened his sorrowful brown eyes, and looked at Brother Stephen. It was a look Brother Stephen knew from somewhere not long ago.

Brother Stephen could stand it no longer. He knelt beside the suffering animal, cradled the buck's head in his hands, and wept bitterly.

"What have I done? Oh God, what have I done to this poor creature?"

And then he remembered the searching look of Brother Bartholomew as he lay dying.

Brother Stephen looked again at the buck. Suddenly there came a voice. "Your pride has caused this harm, my brother."

He wasn't sure if the voice was real or imagined.

"Remember the words of the master: 'For where your treasure is, there shall your heart be also.' The buck would risk all for the simple sweet taste of the apples. His heart was with his treasure. Where is your heart? What is your treasure? What will you risk for the kingdom of God? Or is your heart so sick with the treasure of your own strength that you will trust it, even if you destroy others?"

The words echoed inside Brother Stephen's mind and surrounded his heart till he thought it would burst with shame. He knew the words were true. He looked into the eyes of the great buck.

"I am a fool!" cried Brother Stephen.

"That is true," said the voice, "but knowing that you are a fool is the beginning of wisdom."

With that the buck gave a great snort, raised his head, and struggled to his feet. The creature limped to the gate. He turned back to Brother Stephen, shook his head, pawed, and snorted again.

Brother Stephen walked to the gate, and opened it. As he watched the buck move slowly up the hill, through the silver moonlight and toward the woods, a great rush of light filled his heart and flooded his soul. For the first time since he had come to the monastery, Brother Stephen smiled.

The monks saw a great change in Brother Stephen after that night. First, he took down the barbed wire. And then, though it wasn't easy for him, he left some apples out for the deer. Bad ones at first, but soon the better and best ones. By and by, the fence had holes in it that didn't get fixed and it crumbled more and more. And sometimes, if the truth be told, he left the gate open.

For many years after, the white and pink blossoms of spring turned to rich red and golden apples in the fall. The fallen apples filled the hills around the monastery. Then one day, when Brother Stephen was old and walked with a cane because of his rheumatism, a young monk, Brother Francis, newly come to the monastery, saw the deer eating the apples in the grove. He walked up to Brother Stephen. He wasn't sure if Brother Stephen was praying or sound asleep. He asked him why he didn't take better care of the apple grove.

Brother Stephen raised his head slowly and looked into the eyes of the young monk. Then he looked up the hill to the edge of the woods. There, standing in the shadows, he thought he saw a majestic buck with a golden crown of antlers waiting for him.

Brother Stephen smiled and turned to look at Brother Francis. "God will provide," he said. "He always does."